MUCH ADO
ABOUT
CLUBBiNG

Andrew Fusek Peters
and Polly Peters

To find out more about the authors, visit www.tallpoet.com

This revised version is dedicated to Gary and Rhian Hickey and all
at Ercall Wood School. With thanks for an extraordinary film
premiere of *Much Ado about Clubbing*.

Published in 2008 by
Evans Brothers Ltd
2A Portman Mansions
Chiltern Street
London W1U 6NR

British Library Cataloguing in Publication Data

Peters, Andrew (Andrew Fusek)
    Much ado about clubbing. - (Plays with attitude)
    1. Discotheques - Juvenile drama 2. Children's plays,
    English
    I. Title II. Peters, Polly
    822.9'14

ISBN 9780237534004

Editor: Su Swallow
Designer: Robert Walster, Big Blu Design
Printed in Malta

Cover image istockphoto.com

FOREWORD

Much Ado about Clubbing is something of a cheesy fondue! It melts together deliberate clichés, exaggerated gender stereotypes, puns, wordplay, bizarre props, visual gags, energetic physical theatre and painfully tacky chat-ups. This comic, generally light-hearted piece is played out over the course of an evening at a nightclub. Everyone is there: birthday twins Suzy and Stella; Scott and Jim who hope tonight's the night; girls with attitude; boys who fancy their chances; lonely, over-eager Kenneth and a pair of perfectly synchronised bouncers. In a night out full of twists, melodrama and gender swaps there are also those for whom the club is a sanctuary. Monologues and duologues reveal slices of the lives these individuals want to leave outside. Thus elements of pathos counterbalance the fun and froth.

The play can be used in sections for drama lessons or youth theatre sessions, and provides scope for the imaginative development of scenes. Thus, a few (optional) scenes have instructions for improvisations instead of specified text. Further optional, scripted scenes can be performed or cut in a performance of the whole play, according to time and cast requirements.

Plays with Attitude have been written to appeal to teenage performers and audiences. They are also designed to offer a text-based framework for developing the individual and ensemble physical performance skills explored by students through class-based improvisation. This play is suitable for Key Stages 3 and 4 and sixth form.

CAST LIST

BOUNCER 1: Narrator
BOUNCER 2: Narrator
SUZY: Stella's twin
STELLA: Suzy's twin
JIM: Scott's friend
SCOTT: Jim's friend
MUM
GIRL: Her daughter
KENNETH

GIRLS' GANG:

Not specified by name. Can be played by a smaller or larger number of performers by reallocating lines. Reversed-gender characters should be played either by members of the gangs or by a separate group.
GIRL / 'LAD' 1
GIRL / 'LAD' 2
GIRL / 'LAD' 3
GIRL / 'LAD' 4
GIRL / 'LAD' 5
GIRL / 'LAD' 6

LADS' GANG:

See directions for girls' gang
LAD / 'GIRL' 1
LAD / 'GIRL' 2
LAD / 'GIRL' 3
LAD / 'GIRL' 4

COMMENTATORS 1 & 2: From lads' gang, or separate

NB There are extra roles for girls and lads throughout the play. Depending on the size of the cast they can be played by members of the boys' and girls' gangs or by additional actors.

CHARACTERS IN OPTIONAL SCENES:
LAD, ALONE: Scene 23
LOUNGE LIZARD: Scene 26
TRAINER: Scene 28

Cast requirements: With doubling and reduction of group sizes the play can be performed with a minimum cast of 13. When a large cast is used, roles can be spread out to accommodate up to thirty. Extra non-speaking roles can be created too. All performers can mime (unobtrusively) throughout the club scenes, at the edge of the stage, observing the central action when appropriate.

All wear similar costumes, eg black, except bouncers. Add other clothes and accessories over the top: scarves, jackets, tops, belts, shirts, wrap-around skirts, and jewellery. All should be easy to remove. This is to encourage performers to concentrate on the physical realisation of their characters, rather than relying on costume and make-up, and to enable the gender-swap scenes to be conveyed convincingly through the physical stereotyping of male/female posturing and mannerisms.

Minimal set and props will enable smooth movement between scenes. Small tables, chairs and stools, a coat rack, toy cats and dogs, and buckets are required.

Scene 1

As audience enters, the two bouncers are in role on the door. Half masked, or wearing dark glasses, they can be male or female. They move in unison, checking tickets, making comments on dress code, frisking their friends and family, almost barring entry then relenting.

If using large cast, groups can be in tableaux ranged around the space as audience enters. Appropriate music and lighting.

Bouncers walk onstage when audience settles and become narrators commenting on action. They move in synchronised manner like Siamese twins and speak as one person, alternating lines.

BOUNCER 1: A night out at the club.

BOUNCER 2: Aye! There's the rub.

Both make gestures

BOUNCER 1: Know what I mean?

BOUNCER 2: Let's set the

BOTH:　　scene.

BOUNCER 1: We're the bouncers,

BOUNCER 2: the trouncers.

BOUNCER 1: We're well hard!

BOUNCER 2: Oooof.

BOUNCER 1: We let you

BOUNCER 2: in

BOUNCER 1: or chuck you

BOUNCER 2: out.

BOUNCER 1: In

BOUNCER 2: and

BOUNCER 1: out.

BOUNCER 2: Nicely summed up me old penny, hay-whistle, cock-sparrow, how's your father, cor blimey have a butchers at that!

Girl walks past

BOUNCER 1: You what? But first,

BOUNCER 2: for those who are cursed,

BOUNCER 1: you won't get the hots

BOUNCER 2: unless you... hide those spots.

BOUNCER 1: Dreaming of flesh?

BOUNCER 2: You'd better get fresh-ened up. So-o-o,

BOUNCER 1: mouthwash!

Choreographed movements to match each word/line

BOUNCER 2: Dosh!

BOUNCER 1: Relay-

BOUNCER 2: shunships?

BOUNCER 1: Wiggle

BOUNCER 2: those hips into something new.

Both wolf-whistle

BOUNCER 1: Getting ready,

BOUNCER 2: hold it steady.

BOTH: Let's go

BOUNCER 1: and see the players for this night

BOUNCER 2: prepare the look that seems just right.

BOUNCER 1: We'll kick off the evening by taking a peek

BOUNCER 2: at some of the dreamers and what they seek.
Both exit

Scene 2

Twins Suzy and Stella in their bedroom getting ready. Suzy dances around. Stella is seated. The differences in personality should be shown physically.

SUZY: *[Sings]* Happy birthday to us, happy birthday to us, happy birthday dear u-us...

STELLA: *[Can't stand this]* Yeah, yeah. Whatever. Big night.

SUZY: Oh yes, big night, gonna be great, groovy, wonderful, wunderbar, fab, fantastic...

STELLA: Thank you Suzy, I think we get the point.

SUZY: Matching gear tonight, from beads to bags to bracelets – be hard to tell us apart.

STELLA: Do we have to? Just because we came out of that shared womb minutes apart, oh please, doesn't mean we're Siamese!

SUZY: *[Ignores her]* They'll all be there. Wonder what time Scott and Jim'll arrive?

STELLA: Ah yes. Dim Jim and seriously hot Scott!

SUZY: Stella! That's not fair. Jim's really sweet!

STELLA: Sweet? Oh, really Suzy, pass me the sick bag! It's not a word I associate with 'man'. Now Scott on the other hand... mmm... *[Aside to audience]*
          Let her stick with saddo sweeties,
          Sherbert lolly dabs.
          I prefer a muscle six-pack,
          Drop-dead hunk with awesome abs.

Suzy: [To audience while Stella preens herself]
          Sharp as a stiletto,
          My twin sister Stella.
          Her looks could kill,
          But always get the fella.
          While poor old me
          Can't afford to be choosy,
          It's a lad-free zone
          For Woozy Suzy.

STELLA: Come on then snail, let's quit this jail.

SUZY: This little chick is going free range. Tonight perhaps
          my luck will change! I am... ready!

Both exit, Suzy singing Happy birthday to us etc

STELLA: [From offstage] Will you cut that out and get a
          move on?

Scene 3

Jim and Scott in Scott's bedroom, both getting ready in front of
mimed mirror, stage front, facing audience. Possibly use board-
mounted Star Trek posters on music stands in background to give
context to the boys' Star Trek references.

SCOTT: [Hums Star Trek theme tune as he preens] I think, dear
          Jim boy, we can safely say there are no problems in
          my engine room this evening.

JIM: It's okay for you Scott...

SCOTT: [Shrugs] I know, but then, look at me. I mean, that's
          what girls do: look at me. I just have this certain

warp factor.

JIM: You mean you are warped!

SCOTT: Jim lad, you have to take command of this ship. We neeeeeed to work on you. Girls are an alien species. I've done a lot of study on this subject.

JIM: You mean, you're obsessed and spend a lot of time alone with a computer screen.

SCOTT: Girls! Not life as we know it, Jim.

JIM: But that's my problem. I just don't know what to say half the time.

SCOTT: *[Not listening]* Beam me up totty!

JIM: I mean, Stella. Now, she's out of my orbit, but my legs turn to jelly when I see her and my mouth goes as dry as the sand in the quarg desert of the thirty-third quadrant...

SCOTT: *[Holds up his hand]* Enough! Got the picture. It's clear you need some guidance, from a mate who is cooler than a Vulcan's ice pick.

JIM: You mean, you'll help? If I could just find the right words...

SCOTT: You and me are together on this enterprise, Jim. I'll see what I can do... *[Puts hands round Jim's shoulders, leads him off. Aside to audience]*
           Too sensitive is our lovely Jim,
           Poor boy. I just put up with him.
           He'll never be a life go-getter. *[Sighs, patronising]*
           Makes me look even better!
           Forget him. Now then, how to tell her?
           I'd love to land on Planet Stella!

Exit

Scene 4

Mum and Girl in living room. Mum is ironing.

MUM: No, no. Absolutely no way.

GIRL: Why not?

MUM: Because I'm your mother. What I say goes. And
         you're not going.

GIRL: Mother? That's a joke. When it suits you.

MUM: And what's that supposed to mean?

GIRL: You know what I mean. You don't have a reason, do
         you? You want to spoil any tiny bit of fun I might
         have because you're so miserable yourself. Isn't that
         it? You want me to be just like you, with your sour-
         plum face and your bitter-lemon mouth.

MUM: How dare you talk to me like that? You'll see the
         back of my hand, you will.

GIRL: Go on then. Make you feel better, would it? Take it
         out on me? Instead of on that pathetic, drunken
         mess you call my father.

MUM: Don't you talk about your dad like that. He always
         said spare the rod, spoil the child.

GIRL: Hit a nerve, have I?

MUM: You leave your dad out of this, you hear? He's got his
         own problems. You don't understand.

GIRL: Oh yeah. That's right. Stick up for him, but never for
         me. Doesn't matter what he says or does. Never
         stand up to him. Never on my side.

MUM: It's not a question of sides.

GIRL: Could have fooled me. Anyway, I'm off. Bye,
         'Mother' dear.

MUM: Perhaps you didn't hear me. You. Are. Staying.
         Right. Here.

GIRL: [Stares, challenging] Like. Hell. I. Am. I'm sick of your
         sermons. Truth is you're jealous – jealous 'cos I'm
         young and free and you're old, wrung out and stuck.
         Why don't you just tell him where to stick it, eh?

MUM: You foul-mouthed little... Your dad's right. I don't
         know why I bother.

GIRL: Now it's out. Yeah, Dad is 'right', right off his face.
         Every night.

MUM: Just one more word...

GIRL: And you'll what? Go on, I'm dying to know.

MUM: Get out. Get out of my sight before I...

GIRL: Exactly what I've been trying to do. [Shouts back]
         And don't bother waiting up. [To audience] As if.
         [Storms offstage]

Mum exits

Scene 5

Girls burst onstage, giggling, carrying buckets. Some sit on upturned buckets.

GIRL 6:   Put on some music will you? Let's get in a party mood.

GIRL 1:   *[Holding bucket to side of face]* What am I going to do about this spot?

GIRL 2:   What spot? Can't see a *particular* spot. Can you?

GIRL 3:   Nah! Well, hardly.

GIRL 1:   Really? You don't think anyone will notice?

GIRL 4:   Welllll... perhaps a bit of *[Rummages in bucket, holds up large paintbrush and pot of paint]* concealer will do the trick!

GIRL 5:   Yeah, a dib here, a dab there, no worries!

GIRL 1:   Should I squeeze it first?

GIRL 3:   *[Indrawn breath]* Risky business that.

GIRL 6:   Might need some

GIRL 2:   help!

All gather round bucket spot and mime squeezing

GIRL 1:   Owwww!

ALL: Here it gooooeees! *[Mime fountain-like spurt and all fall backwards]*

GIRL 1:   *[Wiggles head, bucket is still held there]* That's better.

GIRL 5:   Yeah, practically disappeared.

GIRL 6:   *[Wiping hands in disgust]* Just slap on some foundation now. *[Aside]* Complete renovation job if you ask me. Face like a building site.

GIRL 4: There we are.

GIRL 5: Invisible!

GIRL 2: Down to business.

ALL: Let's get beautiful. *[All stand in line. Girl 4 is at the end with cosmetics in bucket]*

GIRL 2: Make-up bag!

GIRL 4: *[Holds up a bucket]* Make-up bag! *[Hands it down the line]*

GIRL 2: Lip-gloss!

GIRL 4: *[Hands lip-gloss down assembly line]* Lip-gloss!

GIRL 1: Eyelash curler!

GIRL 4: Eyelash curler! *[Hands it out]*

GIRL 3: Blusher!

GIRL 4: Blusher!

GIRL 5: Mascara, waterproof.

GIRL 4: Mascara, black, waterproof.

GIRL 6: Nail varnish!

GIRL 4: Nail varnish! And for that final touch, body-glitter!

They begin choreographed, mimed routine of getting ready to music

GIRL 1: Oh we are looking

GIRL 2: fine,

GIRL 3: sultry,

GIRL 4: stunning,

GIRL 5: drop-dead

GIRL 6: gorgeous.

GIRL 3: *[Holds buckets, one each side of head]* These earrings? Too... loud?

All pause to look

GIRL 2: Nah! Knockout baby!

All continue

GIRL 5: *[Turns around, has two buckets with handles over shoulders, worn bra-style]* Whose is this top? Can I borrow it?

GIRL 1: Balconette!

GIRL 2: Looks great!

All ready now. Choreograph actions to suit following words

ALL: Watch out boys, we're heading near.
We're irresistible, it's clear.
Our pulling power is like a net
And what we want, we always get!

All girls pick up buckets in unison, exit with them as handbags

Scene 6

Lads enter, all in front of mimed mirror facing audience. Choreographed movements.

LAD 1: *[Gulps mouthwash]* Say it, don't spray it!

LAD 2: Your breath is not bad. It's evil. You need an exorcism.

LAD 3: You mean Sex**Y**-orcism.

LAD 4:   All I dream of is the kiss of life.

All pucker up lips and give the mirror a kiss

LAD 1:   We need tactics here. Hair!

All gel hair

          Teeth!

All inspect and pick teeth

          Ears!

All stick fingers in ears. One licks finger

ALL: Yeurrgghhh!

LAD 2:   Pits!

All sniff each other's armpits. All sniff Lad 4 and drop dead simultaneously

LAD 4:   They're not that bad. Me 'man'! Woman like 'man' smell. Sweat make sexy, sexy, sexy.

LAD 2:   You mean exit, exit, exit. I can't breathe.

All look in mirror for spots

LAD 1:   Any girl that gets too close to Mr Infestation here would get the kiss of death. *[To Lad 3]* Your boils are bubonic!

LAD 2:   This volcano is about to erupt. This is a major alert. Close the airports. Bring in the army. Sell the movie rights.

LAD 3:   It's not fair! Girls get make-up to cover their spots.

ALL: Ahhhhh!

All smirk in mirror, finish preparations

ALL: Right!

LAD 1:   We

LAD 2:   are

LAD 3:   the

LAD 4:   gang!

LAD 1:   Girl-seeking

LAD 2:   is

LAD 3:   our

LAD 4:   thang!

ALL: We're not nervous,
           Never, no way. [All *shaking knees*]
           We choose to move our legs this way!
           Off to the feast,
           Time for the beast-ly passion play...

Exit

Scene 7

Kenneth enters. Puts on appalling array of clothes.

KENNETH: Soooooooooo excited. Tantalising. My mum said I...
         could... stay... out... LATE! And she doesn't mind,
         not in the least, about bringing back friends for
         choccy biccies. Mmmm. The gang will be there.
         Great to be in the gang. Good guys. They've got lots
         of names for me. Some I don't understand... but it
         will be fun, fun, funtastic. Feeling ready, feeling
         steady, feeling goooood! Soooooooo excited.

Exits

Scene 8

Bouncers enter.

BOUNCER 1: Here we are then,

BOUNCER 2: shoulders squaring.

BOUNCER 1: Doors are

BOUNCER 2: open,

BOUNCER 1: sound is blaring.

BOUNCER 2: Lots inside already

BOUNCER 1: revelling. Mood plus music,

BOUNCER 2: it's

BOTH: bedevilling.

BOUNCER 1: We, the bouncers, feeling frisky. *[Frisk each other]*

BOUNCER 2: Watch the chat-ups

BOUNCER 1: getting

BOUNCER 2: risky.

BOUNCER 1: Say what you think!

BOUNCER 2: Have a

BOUNCER 1: drink. Cheers!

BOUNCER 1: Lose your fears.

BOUNCER 2: Lose yourself.

BOUNCER 1: Acne squats under make-

BOUNCER 2: up's

BOTH: shelf.

BOUNCER 1: Recycle your

BOUNCER 2: old reality.

BOUNCER 1: Buy yourself a new per-

BOUNCER 2: son-

BOUNCER 1: ality.

BOUNCER 2: Go on,

BOUNCER 1: enjoy it.

BOUNCER 2: Take a chance,

BOUNCER 1: ask for a dance.

BOUNCER 2: Over there, he understands

BOUNCER 1: how to moo-oo-oove

BOTH: those hands. *[Mime arms inching across girl's shoulder]*

BOUNCER 1: Heaving palace of

BOUNCER 2: getting together.

BOUNCER 1: So come on in, it's now or

BOTH: never. *[Become serious once more, back in work mode]*

Scene 9

Three of girls' gang enter club. Appropriate music and lighting. Girl 2 enters in front. Girl 1 and Girl 3 behind. Throughout first part of scene, Girl 2 strives to make an impression: tosses hair, smoothes clothes, swings hips etc. Girls 1 and 3 mimic her, exaggerating wildly behind her back. They stop and look innocent each time she turns.

GIRL 2:   Not many here yet. Oh, couple of nice lads over by the bar though. *[Looks across, offstage]*

GIRL 1:   Oooooh yeah! Blonde alert! I like them fair.

GIRL 3:   It's the wallet that counts, girl. Forget the hair.

GIRL 2:   And what's under the t-shirt.

GIRL 1:   Definitely! I'll have the six-pack to take out, please.

GIRL 2:   So where shall we head for? I want the best view.

GIRL 3:   *[Looks at Girl 2's back]* Oh, I think we've got that already, don't you?

They giggle, copying Girl 2's unusual posture

GIRL 2:   Where?

GIRL 1:   Um, oh... over there.

Girls 1 and 3 continue to mimic and stifle giggles as they copy Girl 2

GIRL 2:   What is it?

GIRL 3:   Nothing.

They all walk

GIRL 2:   You sure?

GIRLS 1 & 3: Oh yes!

They walk

GIRL 2:   Come on... what? *[She catches them out]* I saw that! You... *[She tries to look offended and keep a straight face but cracks and giggles. They all laugh]* cheeky cows! I'll get you for that.

Girls 4, 5 & 6 rush in and catch them up. Girl 4 has bucket over her head. Lifts it so mouth is visible

GIRL 4:   Just stopped to touch up our make-up. D'you think I slapped on a bit too much?

GIRL 1:   Course not. You look lovely. Nice and subtle. *[Aside to Girl 3]* Why use a spade when a JCB will do?

GIRL 5:   *[Holds bucket to backside and turns sideways]* But really, be honest. Was skintight a mistake? Does it make my bum look big?

ALL: *[Nod heads]* Noooo!

GIRL 6: I keep telling you, it's tiny, OK?

GIRL 5: OK, if you say so. *[Turns again and knocks Girl 3 sideways with bucket/bum]*

GIRL 3: Oooofff!

GIRL 6: Come on then you lot. Where's the action? *[Music changes]* Ooooh this is my favourite.

GIRL 4: Let's go for it girls.

Move to back, use buckets as handbags to dance around

Scene 10

Lads enter and make their way to bar.

LAD 1: Of course, you've just got to act nonchalant.

LAD 2: Nonchalant, right? Just watch me go into action.

LAD 3: Who you gonna go for?

LAD 4: What you gonna say?

LAD 2: It's all in the book, boys. *[Holds up small book]*

LAD 1: *[Reads aloud]* 'From the Snog to the Whole Hog', by I.M. Showvin Istpiggman.

LAD 2: It's got loads of great lines. Look. *[To Lad 4]* Pretend you're a girl.

LAD 3: That won't be hard.

LAD 4: Knock it off.

LAD 2: *[Said with predatory look]* Is that a ladder in your tights, sweetheart, or just a stairway to heaven?

LAD 4: *[Falsetto]* Oh... my, I'm in lurvvvve.

LAD 3: Their tongues will be hanging out... not.

LAD 1: So original.

LAD 2: Yeah, but that's the point. They're not gonna know that. They might even think I'm a sensitive poet.

LAD 4: About as sensitive as sandpaper.

LAD 2: Well I'm not scared. At least I'm daring enough to give it a go. See that group over there? The one in the middle. *[Points at girls' group]* Watch and learn, little boys. Watch and learn. *[Swaggers over to girls, finally manages to get appointed girl's attention. Coughs, obviously trying to remember his line. Music grows louder. He shouts into her ear]* Did it hurt when you fell down from heaven?

GIRL 1: What?

LAD 2: Did it hurt...

GIRL 1: What?

LAD 2: *[Yells]* Did it hurt... when you fell down from heaven?

GIRL 1: What? You've hurt yourself and your name's Stefan?

LAD 2: No I haven't and no it's not!

GIRL 1: Snot. Stefan Snot! Oh my gawd! You poor darling!

All girls giggle and point at him

LAD 2: Oh never mind. *[Comes back to lads]*

LAD 1: A great start to the evening. Ditch the book, boy, and get us another drink.

All move to side

Scene 11

Girl from Scene 4, spotlit.

GIRL: My mum could part the flaming waves with her
        voice. Going on about where I go and who I hang
        out with and of course, every boy is the evil one
        himself. She makes a simple night out sound like
        Sodom and Gomorrah. And my dad? On his knees as
        usual, worshipping the bleeding bottle. He's turned
        my mum's heart into a pillar of salt. If he isn't
        snoring, or slurring, he's snapping at me, calling me
        a *slapper*, for wanting a bit of fun. Hypocrite. I have
        to get them off my case, get to see my mates, get *out*.
        This is no den of iniquity here. It's my promised land:
        church of chat-up where I pray to score just a little
        affection. I love the cheesiness – dress as loud as you
        want – collars that could meet each other round the
        back and skirts that are easily mistaken for a collar...
        The ebb and flow of gossip is a river. In the loos,
        doors swing like confessionals – who told on who and
        who said what. This is a cool communion. Up all
        night to dance the hurt of home away. It's just me in
        my wake-up make-up, my mates and my music... If
        only I could meet a miracle. Nights like this? I pray
        they never end.

Moves away

Scene 12

Suzy and Stella enter.

SUZY: Oh good, lots of people here already.

STELLA: Well, we wouldn't have wanted to get here early, would we? How horribly uncool.

SUZY: Look. Everyone's over there. *[Points to girls]* Come on.

STELLA: Not exactly my definition of 'everyone', but they'll do to start with. Do you have to look so eager? *[They have reached girls]* Hi!

Girls all gather round them and improvise, greeting and shouting 'Happy birthday' raucously and making a fuss of them

GIRL 2:   We've got something for you.

GIRL 1:   Yeah! We all clubbed together. *[To Girl 4]* Where did you put it all?

GIRL 4:   Didn't it go in someone's handbag?

GIRL 1:   Did it? Whose?

GIRL 4:   Bear with us a minute you two.

SUZY: Oh, you shouldn't have bothered, really.

STELLA: *[Under breath]* Believe me, I'm wishing you hadn't.

Girls search through buckets, holding up an assortment of odd and humorous contents in the process

           Oh God, how embarrassing. Is anyone looking?

SUZY: What? Don't be silly. Does it matter?

GIRL 3:   Here we are! *[Holds up presents]*

GIRL 5:   Knew they were here somewhere. *[Helps carry them]*

GIRL 6:   Go on, open them. Oooh, I love birthdays!

Suzy and Stella unwrap identical clothes and/or accessories, which they put on, and identical party hats. Each hat has their name in large letters on the front

GIRL 6:   So, what do you think?

GIRL 5:   Do you like them?

GIRL 1:   So we can tell you apart.

SUZY: Oh thank you! Thanks everyone! I love the hat, don't you Stella?

STELLA: Yeah! Yeah! Whatever makes you happy. *[To girls]* Thank you. So thoughtful.

GIRL 2:   Oooh, look who's just arrived.

Scott and Jim enter

            They're heading this way!

GIRL 5:   But it's not us they're making for.

GIRL 3:   We'll leave you to it then, shall we?

SUZY: Catch you all later. Thanks again.

Girls' gang makes way to side of stage

Scene 13

Scott and Jim approach.

SCOTT: All right Stella! Oh, hi Suzy. Happy birthday both. Hey, love the hats!

JIM: Yeah, er... me too.

STELLA: They were presents.

SCOTT: Oh? Presents? Sorry. Should have thought. But you can have the benefit of my lovely lips. Here's a birthday kiss for you Stella! *[Kisses her cheek. Catches Jim's eye]* Oh, and one for you too Suzy.

JIM: Er... er having a good night?

STELLA: Yeah. Goodnight! *[Turns to talk to Scott]* So, you going to offer us a drink then, cheapskates? Or are you going to let two lovely ladies stand here with nothing to hold? *[She mimes tilting a glass]*

SCOTT: You can always hold me... oh. Hey, it's Jim's round! He's the generous one. Why don't you go with him and choose what you want?

STELLA: Oh, all right.

JIM: Great! Er... this way then. Er... *[Sees Suzy about to follow]* Shall we choose for you Suzy?

SUZY: Oh, OK. *[She watches Jim's retreating back]*

SCOTT: Yeah, that's right. You stay here with me Suze.

SUZY: Suzy.

SCOTT: Yeah, whatever. Um... your twin, your sister. She's something, isn't she?

SUZY: Is she?

SCOTT: Oh, I'm not saying you're not. You're just... different. You have different and wonderful qualities, both of you. But Stell, well, how do you get to grips with someone like her? You know her better than anyone. What would... impress her... get her attention?

SUZY: Oh, I think you're capable of making all the right moves Scott. You seem to be doing fine so far.

SCOTT: I do? I mean... oh... here they are. That was quick.

Jim and Stella arrive with drinks

        Thanks.

STELLA: Hold mine, Suzy, I want crisps.

SCOTT: Oh, wait, I'll get them! Here, Jim, look after this!

Hands drink back. Scott and Stella move away

JIM: Right. *[Looks round for somewhere to put drinks down, but there isn't anywhere. He hovers nervously]* Er, looks like it's going to be a great evening. *[Nervous pause]* Having a good birthday? *[Cranes round trying to see Scott and Stella]*

SUZY: *[Eager]* Oh yes! What do you think of these? *[Points to hat]* They're fun aren't they! The girls made them, and they gave us this stuff too, and, well, things are looking up even more now you've both got here.

JIM: *[Not listening]* Right. Er... Suzy, can I ask you something?

SUZY: Yes? *[Looks expectant]*

JIM: About Stella?

SUZY: Oh...

JIM: Well, I'd really like to make a good impression; do something that would make me, you know, stand out. That sort of thing.

SUZY: I see.

JIM: Scott's promised to help. In fact, he's probably working on it now.

SUZY: I'm sure he is.

JIM: So, what else should I do?

SUZY: Jim, I... well, I... I'm not sure... Let me think... Oh look! They're calling us over. Must want those. *[Points to drinks]*

JIM: Oh... sure, of course, better oblige then. But... you will let me know won't you... if there's anything specific?

SUZY: *[Sighs]* Yes.

They move to back

Scene 14

Girls' group moves centre-stage.

GIRL 5: I'm off to the loo. Who's coming?

GIRL 1: Me!

GIRL 4: Oi, you lot – loo trip!

GIRL 3: OK, just a moment.

GIRL 2: I'm coming.

GIRL 6: Let's go.

They link arms and move stage right, giggling and improvising snippets of conversation. Mime entering toilets. Place three buckets on floor as toilets and three on chairs as washbasins. Reapply make-up, brush hair etc., while improvising gossipy chat. Lights fade on loos and spotlight comes up on lads, stage left

LAD 2: Back in a minute, uh, where's the bogs?

LAD 1: *[Gestures vaguely]* Over there mate.

LAD 2: Uh, right. *[Moves stage right. Stops outside girls' toilets, peers round]* Must be this one. *[Mimes entering. Does double take as realises where he is]*

Girls squeal as Lad 2 enters, then laugh and close tightly round him

GIRL 4:   My, my. What have we got here?

LAD 2:   *[Tries to push back through them]* Er... er...

GIRL 1:   Where do you think you're going?

LAD 2:   Er... sorry... Er... *[Looks frantic]*

GIRL 2:   Did de 'ickle boy get lost den? *[Tries to pinch his cheek]*

LAD 2:   Mistake. Got it wrong. Right?

GIRL 3:   Or did you just want a good look, eh?

LAD 2:   Wha...? No, look... wrong door, that's all.

GIRL 6:   This is a urinal free zone, darling.

LAD 2:   I'll just go then.

GIRL 5:   Well, we all have to 'go' don't we girls? *[Laughs]* Be our guest. *[She points towards a toilet. Girls laugh]* And then we'll see what you're made of.

GIRL 3:   How much of a 'man' you are! *[Reaches towards him]*

GIRLS: Phwoooarrr!

LAD 2:   Aaarghhhh! *[Breaks through circle and exits. Stands outside mimed door]* That was too much. *[Looks around again, walks round to other side of loos, finds another door]* Phew. *[Enters girls' toilets again! They have backs to him. He walks towards toilet, then stops, does double-take as girls turn round]* What the...?

GIRL 2:   Back so soon?

GIRL 6:   Can't keep away, can he?

Lad 2 backs away towards door

GIRL 4:   *[Runs between him and door]* Two doors, duh. One for each dance floor.

GIRLS 1 & 4: Didn't you know?

GIRL 1:   One each side. *[Points to doors]*

LAD 2:   Ooooooh noooo! Let me go!

GIRL 5:   Still not 'gone' love? Ooooh, you must be desperate by now!

GIRL 3:   Poor thing.

GIRL 4:   This way! *[She twirls him round]*

GIRL 2:   Or this way? *[She catches him and spins him]*

Girls spin him between them like pinball machine

LAD 2:   Oh, God! Just let me... No, give me a chance to... Get off me!

GIRL 5:   Hey! He says he wants to GET OFF with me!

LAD 2:   No, I... arghhhh! *[He breaks away and runs out with Girl 5 in pursuit as far as door]*

GIRL 5:   *[Shouts after him]* Come back lover boy, what have 'weeeee' got to 'loos'?

Girls collapse together in hysterics then exit with buckets

Scene 15

Lights come up centre stage on Girl standing alone. Nervous Lad sidles up to her.

NERVOUS LAD: Do you come here a lot?

GIRL: No.

NERVOUS LAD: Do you live round here, then?

GIRL: No.

NERVOUS LAD: So, you here with anyone special?

GIRL: No.

NERVOUS LAD: *[Excited]* Have you got a boyfriend?

GIRL: No.

NERVOUS LAD: Great. I mean. You're so... well, well. Do you want to... dance?

GIRL: No.

NERVOUS LAD: Oh. Was it something I said?

GIRL: No.

NERVOUS LAD: You don't say a lot, do you?

GIRL: No.

NERVOUS LAD: In fact, I don't stand a chance with you, do I?

GIRL: No.

NERVOUS LAD: Right, I'll errr... be off then.

GIRL: Yes!

Both freeze. Lads 2 and 3 step forward, acting as football commentators to respond to last scene. Remote control in the hands of Lad 2

LAD 2:   Let's see that again in slow motion Ron...

Nervous Lad moves slowly up to Girl to begin questions

LAD 3:   Yes, he's moving up the left field. The ball's in his control.

LAD 2:   You can say that again, Ron.

LAD 3:   The ball's in his control! And he shoots off the question.

NERVOUS LAD: *[Lines and actions replayed very slowly with deep voices]* Dooo yooou commme heeere aaa lotttt?

GIRL: Noooo.

Both continue miming slowly

LAD 2:   Oh no!

LAD 3:   Awful pass!

LAD 2:   Let's just freeze it there

Nervous Lad and Girl freeze

           and go back a bit.

Nervous Lad and Girl move and speak backwards, as in reverse action replay or film being played backwards

GIRL: Ooon.

NERVOUS LAD: Tolll aaaa eerreeeeh eemoc uuoooooy ooooood.

LAD 3:   Real Men United will be very disappointed with this poor showing.

Lad walks away backwards

LAD 2:   Just couldn't score the girl, erm goal... Over to you, Ron!

LAD 3:   Well, let's just try a little fantasy replay shall we?

Take a look at this. *[Presses remote control]*

Nervous Lad becomes a commanding hero who swiftly approaches the girl and speaks in a deeper, melodramatic voice as he mimes the fantasy

NERVOUS LAD: Carruthers took her by the hand. Forcefully, he pressed himself upon her. 'Would you like this dance?' he muttered. She uttered a sigh.

GIRL: Yes! Yes! Yes!

NERVOUS LAD: His strong arms took her to the floor. Hip to hip, a man and a woman moving to the heat of the primal rhythm, their bodies crying out to each other for more than just a

GIRL AND NERVOUS LAD: syn-co-pa-tion!

GIRL: Oh Carruthers!

NERVOUS LAD: Oh Cecilia!

GIRL: *[Passionately]* Oh Carruthers!

NERVOUS LAD: *[Even more passionately]* Oh Cecilia!

They embrace. Other two lads clap, shouting 'Bravo!' 'Jolly good show!' 'That's more like it,' etc.

LAD 3:   Uh, you can stop now. *[Presses remote]* Stop, I said stop. Stop!

They freeze

OK. As you were.

They turn away from each other and walk away

LAD 2:   Ah well, fun to dream.

Exit

Scene 16

Stella alone. Scott approaches and points to her hat.

SCOTT: Ah, there you are, my steely Stella. Wasn't sure for a moment if it was you or Suzy.

STELLA: Do you mind? Anyway, Suzy's busy being woozy somewhere – just a sip of something fizzy does go to her head, poor thing.

SCOTT: While you, on the other hand, could drink even me under the table, eh Stella?

STELLA: Oh Scott, I don't think I'd need a drink to get you under the table!

SCOTT: *[Flustered for a second]* Woah, so, er, tell me, what is it you look for in a man?

STELLA: I'm looking right now. Just don't give me any of that roses in the teeth, spouting soppy love poetry yuck stuff. That's Woozy's handbag, not mine. I prefer pulling power to poetry any day.

SCOTT: I'll bear that in mind.

STELLA: I hope you'll bare more than your mind to me, Scott. The question is: is Scott scot-free right now?

SCOTT: Phew. Oh he is, Stella. He is, I... is, am. But first, I have a little bit of business to attend to. I'll be back quicker than a... really quick thing. So, until later, put those lips in a parking spot, and I'll be back to read your meter. *[Scott moves backwards, still looking stunned, mesmerized by Stella]*

A lad pogos across the stage, knocking into Scott

SCOTT: Ooof. What the hell are you doing?

LAD: Me? I'm the bouncer, right! Any trouble and I'll...
          boing, boing, boing!

*He bounces on spot until the two real bouncers approach from each
side. Lad stops bouncing. Bouncers pick him up by the elbows
silently and carry him off. Scott and Stella melt into club background*

Scene 17

*Groups and pairs of clubbers are ranged around the stage, miming
socialising together. Kenneth enters and approaches each group/
individual in turn. In his desire to be part of things, his actions and
mannerisms are excruciatingly over-the-top and exaggerated.*

KENNETH: Me me me me me, my oh my, I'm the party animal,
         me. Party, party, party all night long. I am the life
         and soul. Just love to, have to, need to talk and
         tittle-tattle, prattle. *[Said up close into someone's face.
         They turn away]* And prate, I just love to, love to
         relate! *[Half hugs someone]* How are you?

Person draws breath, about to speak. Kenneth interrupts

         Oh! Good, goody, giddy, great. I'm great too. Just
         great. Great night out. Must ring. Must meet up. No
         time to chat, must go now.

Person nods, relieved

         Mingle, mingle, mingle. *[Confronts girl and holds her*

arm] My, my, my girl, you are looking good, good gracious, gorgeous, girlfriends ha! Hanging off my arm. Need a bodyguard to beat them off!

Eventually, girl succeeds in wrenching her arm away. Kenneth mimes boxing as though making a joke of it but accidentally punches her on shoulder. She slaps him

Oh no! Didn't mean it, just a jape, joke, a bit of a jolly josh, you know. *[Now wanders as people avoid him]* Never, never alone. Lonely in this palace of people? Moi? I am surrounded. *[Adopts accent and marches]* Surrender all your friendships forthwith! I've got so many friends. They always pop round. Pop, pop, pop! *[Actions become increasingly manic. He runs up to people who scatter]* Call me Kenneth – Ken's your man. Never a problem at a party. Walking phrasebook, go-between for words and wit. I'm with it, with you? *[Approaches one person at a time]* With you? With you? *[Approaches an embracing couple]* Together with you? Oh that's so nice. You've got together. *[He pats their heads. Pulls cheeks]* Don't they look lovely? We all need someone, sometime, somewhere. *[Sings]* Somewhere over the rainbow. Yes indeed, little bit needy.

Couple turn away, ignoring him. Kenneth twists round them, still trying to entwine himself in their embrace and watching them closely

Ooooh. I like the look of that. Tongue twister! Mmmm! Like to try that one-day. But I know all about it, of course. Practise in my spare time. *[Mimes kissing]* Not that I've got any spare time. Buzz, buzz, buzz, such a busy bee. *[Spotlight on Kenneth]* Me me me, oh my, the life... and soul.

Retreats to side

Scene 18

Suzy centre stage.

SUZY: 'Stella this' and 'Stella that'.
I'm sick of wearing the sidekick hat;
Forever shivering in her shade,
The stone for Stella's witty blade.
Meet my twin, we look the same,
But play a very different game.
If I am sweet, then she is sour,
But she's the one who wields the power.
Well, just for once, for one night only,
I won't put up with being lonely.
I have a scheming master plan
To change the rules and win the man.
The taste of plotting is so sweet
To catch a real birthday treat. *[Approaches Stella,
who has been standing, looking bored with Jim]* I need
the loo. Come on, your mascara's smudged. *[To Jim]*
Back in a minute.

STELLA: Now, behave yourself while we're gone and be a
good little boy and see if you can find out where
Scott's got to. *[To Suzy as they walk]* Thank you for
rescuing me! Still, just can't help having them both
at my feet.

SUZY: Well, careful you don't tread on them then.

*They enter toilets, standing at front of stage as if mirror is between
them and audience*

STELLA: Oh, Suzy, you're too considerate. It's your biggest failing. Have you seen the way Jim looks at me with those lost-puppy eyes? Vomit-worthy! *[Touches up make-up]*

SUZY: *[Dreamily]* He's got lovely eyes. *[Takes off her hat and brushes hair]*

STELLA: Not! What planet are you on? He's so gawky.

SUZY: Sensitive.

STELLA: Gawky. Anyway, why are you sticking up for him?

SUZY: Oh dunno. Just think that you don't look at people very closely. Shall I do your hair?

STELLA: What? Oh, OK.

SUZY: *[Removes Stella's hat, puts it next to her own]* It's just like when we were little, isn't it? Doing each other's hair...

STELLA: Was I really ever little? I want to be this age forever.

SUZY: Well, come on then. Let's go celebrate being 'this age'. There. *[Pats Stella's hair]*

Stella exits towards door

Ooh, hang on, don't forget this, Ms Party Animal. *[She puts the hat labelled 'Suzy' on Stella and lets Stella exit ahead]* So it's farewell Suzy *[Waves at Stella's back]* and hello Stella! *[She shows Stella's hat]* I'll be Queen of Hearts and get the fella! *[She puts on Stella's hat, name at front, checks in mirror, then turns it, so name is at back]* Don't want suspicion that anything's strange, so, it's time for a personality change!

Exits

Scene 19

Girl from Scene 4 is sitting alone at table. Kenneth approaches.

KENNETH: My oh my. A lady. Lovely lady lurking all alone. Hello, hello, hello, How are you?

GIRL: All right, I suppose.

KENNETH: Tell me, what is your star sign? What do they call you? Tell tale, tattle what's your name?

GIRL: You haven't really got the hang of this chat-up thing, have you? My dad calls me all sorts of things, but I prefer Sammy.

KENNETH: Play it again Sammy. *[Stands very close to Girl]* Will I get jammy with Sammy? My name, my name, my kingdom for the name of Kenneth with a kicking K.

GIRL: Kenneth. You seem to be great at talking, but I need someone to listen.

KENNETH: Oh but I lurve listening. It's lovely. So much to hear. My ears are yours! *[He flaps them]*

GIRL: Erm right. I don't think this is going to work out, eh?

KENNETH: But I was so close, within a smidgen of a hug. Snuggly, snuggly. *[Rubs his shoulders up against her]* We could be good. Oooooh so good. You and me and me and I. Just give me a chance? Dance? *[Grabs her hands. He dances while she remains passive]* Goodness great. I'm reeeeeeally great...

GIRL: *[She pushes him off]* You are grating on my nerves Kenneth. I don't know how to say this but...

KENNETH: *[Suddenly serious]* I know. 'Bog off.' *[He sighs]* Oh... flip. Story of my life. So, there we go. That's just the way it is. Kenneth... loser.

GIRL: No, you're not, it's just... I've had a hard time at home and...

KENNETH: *[Tries again]* Yes, I could help... to chit, chat, chatter, pitter-patter, cheer you up? No, no, no? Okey dokey. Got the message in a bottle. So many friends to see, I'll just... *[Starts to back off]* just, just...

GIRL: Bye Kenneth.

Kenneth moves away

I pray for a miracle and what do I get? A creepy horror movie! Though I do feel sorry for the guy. Mummy's boy, I reckon. But I bet *his* mum fusses over him, bakes him little cupcakes and makes sure he wears his thermo-fleece vest when he goes out. Sweet, but with all the pulling power of a pair of damp socks. What an evening. If it isn't Kenneth with his toe-curling attempts at conversation, then it's clumsy, drunken yobs, perfect younger mirrors of my dad. At least Kenneth was chatty. This lot just slobber and come up with startling and original lines like, 'Haven't I seen you somewhere before?' 'Like, no.' And the thing is, they don't actually seem to realize that such a predictable line bellowed up close along with a good spray of spit and the odd undigested fleck of steak and kidney landing in your face with a waft of ten-pints-down-the-gullet breath that's more than bad, it's a sewer stinking up your nostrils, is surprisingly, and girls worldwide will back me up on this one, not such a turn on after all! Isn't that right?

[Following text optional]

Oh, but it's amazing what alcohol can achieve. It ought to win prizes. It lowers inhibitions, gets rid of shyness, makes boring macho gits into... even more boring, pathetic gits, if that were possible. In fact, it should be rebranded as the ultimate camouflage kit. For even the puniest, wouldn't know a muscle if it shook his hand at a party and said 'Hello, I'm Mister Bicep,' foul-mouthed, inconsiderate, insensitive, 'isn't a *feeling* what you do with your hands?' oaf – once he's had a couple (and he is dreaming of coupling) – voila! Shake the liver-diseased rabbit out of the hat and suddenly he's under the illusion (delusion) that he's the James Bond of seduction, arriving gift-wrapped from God, somewhere near you. I come here to get away from everything. But there's no forgetting. This country is drowning in drink. A flood of spirits washing away happy families... I wonder how many kids here have hidden drunks in their cupboards. Oh well... God I need a drink. *[Raises her hand to order a drink]*

Spotlight fades. Exits

Scene 20

Lad 1 approaches Suzy from behind, after seeing hat.

LAD 1:   *[Checks the name on back of hat]* Fancy a drink, Stell?

SUZY: I'm not St-stir-crazy about a drink right now, thanks.

Pause. Silence

LAD 1:   You seem quiet. Your sister's usually the quiet one.

SUZY: Oh her. Yeah. Chalk and cheese on the inside, us. *[She begins to get into her stride, pretending to be Stella, flirting]* No, I was just thinking actually, about some serious action... thinking about...

Lad 1 looks hopeful

       Scott, that is.

LAD 1:   Oh. *[Disappointed]* Okay. I'll leave you to it then.

SUZY: Right. Yeah. Cool.

Lad 1 backs away

       Phew.

STELLA: *[Comes up]* What did he want with you?

SUZY: You know, Stella, there are other girls in this world, apart from you.

STELLA: Can't say I've noticed. But, you know, it's odd, the lads don't seem to be paying me their usual attention... *[Looks around]* I don't know why.

SUZY: *[Aside]* Now she knows how it feels. Happy birthday, sis. *[To Stella]* They're probably just intimidated by how good you look tonight.

STELLA: That must be it. It's hard being me sometimes.

SUZY: Really?

STELLA: And where the hell has Scott got to?

Girl 1 comes up, immediately starts talking to Suzy

GIRL 1:   I tell you what, there's some hot action in here
            tonight. You gonna grab any?

STELLA: *[Butts in]* Too right. I am *in* the mood.

GIRL 1:   *[Looks at hat, not at Stella. Looks shocked]* You're in...
            the mood? I didn't know you had it in you.

STELLA: What?

SUZY: *[Whispers to Girl 1]* Don't worry, one too many sips of
            the old birthday bubbles I think.

*Girl 1 laughs and Suzy links arms with her, pulling her away. Stella
looks bewildered. Girl 1 exits. Scott and Jim enter from opposite
sides at the back. Both are scanning the room at head height and spot
Suzy's hat. They each move straight past Stella who looks even more
bewildered. She shakes her head as Scott reaches Suzy first, then
storms offstage*

SCOTT: There you are. All right my little pancake, fancy
            cooking up something sweet?

SUZY: I couldn't give a toss about pancakes, Scotty!

SCOTT: What? Only a joke.

SUZY: Yes you are, but you'll never know. *[Turns away
            towards Jim who has just arrived at her side]*

SCOTT: But what about... about...

JIM: Er... I'd like to talk to you later, if you're around.

SUZY: A round! That's a good idea. Scott, get us a round in
            then. I'll have a coke.

SCOTT: Sure, anything you say Stell. Blimey.

SUZY: *[To Jim]* You can talk to *me* anytime you want.

JIM: Oh, great. Right then. *[Nervous]* I'll just help Scott with the drinks. Back in a bit. All right?

They exit

SUZY: *[Aside]* Oh, he is a bit of all right that Jim. Just slightly cross-eyed, under the spell of the not-so-lovely Stell... I'm quite enjoying all this attention. Does wonders for the confidence. *[Pats hat]* All that difference just in a name – and a way of behaving. We'll see...

Exits

Scene 21

Bouncers step forward.

BOUNCER 1: Poor old Jim.

BOUNCER 2: Wants Stell to love *him*.

BOUNCER 1: She's got this boy by the

BOUNCER 2: short and curly.

BOUNCER 1: He thinks she's the one –

BOUNCER 2: most superior girly.

BOUNCER 1: But sneaky Scott's got the perfect plan.

BOUNCER 2: If it works, he reckons

BOTH: *he'll* be the man!

Bouncers step back

Scene 22

Jim and Scott by the bar.

JIM: But I'm desperate! I'll try anything!

SCOTT: Desperate? Yes. Well, look Jim, you are captain of this enterprise in destiny and what's more, I've been doing a bit of undercover work.

JIM: You mean under *the* cover...

SCOTT: Good one! Seriously, you need something to grab Stella by the... proverbials.

JIM: I'm waiting.

SCOTT: Well, a little birdy-wirdy told me that our ice-cool Stell is secretly longing for the roses and romantic poem treatment.

JIM: Stella and sonnets? That's like Star Trek meets Balamory. *[Or other current children's TV programme]* You're joking!

SCOTT: *[Aside]* Precisely! *[To Jim]* You need to trust me on this. We're getting to grips with her sensitive side, the fluffy bunny within. You get the picture? Do the old down-on-your-knees business and she is absolutely guaranteed yours. Anyway, you're always 'Larkin' about with that poetry stuff. It's more than my 'Wordsworth'. Go on, think of one. You can do it.

JIM: Oh yeah, poem for every occasion, me! But hang on... there is one I know a bit of. How does it go? 'Come live with me and be... yeah... my love. And we shall all... the pleasures prove.'

SCOTT: Pleasures prove? Now we're talking! Phwoarrr! If I was a girl, my tongue would be scraping the dance floor by now.

JIM: 'That hills and valleys, dales and fields
And all the craggy mountain yields...' Oh, yeah, it's all coming back...

SCOTT: Excellent. Go off somewhere quiet and practise.

Exit

Scene 23

Optional scene. Lad, Alone in club by bar, alone.

LAD ALONE: I make sure I don't stand out, that there's nothing camp about me. And no, there isn't anything out of the ordinary in my background – just dull and drab like everyone else. *[Sighs]* No, I never played with dolls either or dressed up in my sister's clothes... But if anyone at school *knew*, I'd be so dead. I'm sick of it. Politicians and pop stars can talk about it. But in class, if any lad shows even a hint of a single, snotty tear, he's a 'poof'. He'd better not go alone into the bogs after that if he doesn't want to have every feeling he's ever had battered and kicked right out of him. And then if he's seen hanging out with girls, being generally friendly, not trying to get off with any of them, he's definitely 'queer', or just 'girl'. Since when has the word 'girl' been an insult? At least girls talk. It's all macho crap out there – everyone toeing the line. Fags – the type you smoke, fashion, football – haven't seen many footballers come out... though they're always damn well hugging and kissing each other. Well, this is my closet. Here, I can peer round the door. Everyone is daring to be different. So why not me, eh, for a change? I can't be the only one. But for now, I'll act the lad, maybe even get the girl at the end of the night, and they'll all sing 'For he's a jolly good fellow...' That's all I want: a jolly good fellow.

Spot fades

Scene 24

Bouncers step forward.

BOUNCER 1: Let's pause, take stock of

BOUNCER 2: lows and

BOUNCER 1: highs.

BOUNCER 2: This is an evening of

BOUNCER 1: disguise.

BOUNCER 2: Plots are twisting, tightly

BOUNCER 1: turning. Feelings full

BOUNCER 2: and passions burning.

BOUNCER 1: Double-crossing,

BOUNCER 2: bold deception. Night fills up

BOUNCER 1: with mis-

BOUNCER 2: perception. There's magic, drifting

BOUNCER 1: in the air. Enchantment weaving

BOUNCER 2: to ensnare.

BOUNCER 1: Observers

BOUNCER 2: of misrule

BOTH: we two.

BOUNCER 1: We'll add

BOUNCER 2: some mischief to this stew.

BOUNCER 1: *[Pulls a teen magazine from his back pocket with a flourish and flaps the pages, bird-like]* Is this what girls are really reading?

BOUNCER 2: Broken hearts all torn and bleeding!

BOUNCER 1: Tacky tales, celeb hot hype.

BOUNCER 2: What a dose of stereo-tripe!

BOUNCER 1: But it conjures up a wicked plan:

BOUNCER 2: transfiguration!

BOUNCER 1: Do you think we can?

BOUNCER 2: Let's switch things so they're

BOUNCER 1: topsy-turvy.

BOUNCER 2: Girls turn macho.

BOUNCER 1: Lads get curvy.

BOUNCER 2: So...

BOUNCER 1: we'll spread bewitchment, *[Mimes conjuring]*

BOUNCER 2: swap the gender: *[Mimes sleight of hand]*

BOUNCER 1: Girls so

BOUNCER 2: hard

BOUNCER 1: and lads so

BOUNCER 2: tender.

BOTH: Ahhhhh!

What follows is a gender swap where girls act out stereotypes of being lads and lads do the same for girls. There should be maximum physical exaggeration and mimicry in order to make the clichés humorous and blatant. Each performer must completely rework the way they move.

'Lads' and 'girls' groups form. All obvious gender specific clothes/ accessories should be removed or swapped, leaving plain costumes underneath. Each group adopts a tableau which represents lad and girl stereotypes. Bouncers click fingers. Groups come to life and eye each other up. Optional scenes can be improvised by each group.

'LAD' 1:   *[To one of 'girls']* Oi love, come an' feel up these muscles.

Two 'lads' compare biceps

'LAD' 2:   Yeah, an' when you've done that, you can test drive my love muscle. No charge.

'Girls' giggle coyly

'GIRL' 1:   Cheeky!

'GIRL' 2:   *[Approaches 'Lad' 2, feels muscle]* Call that a muscle, lovey? I've seen bigger, pickled in a jar.

'Girls' laugh

'LAD' 3:   Oi. Watch it you or someone might mistake your mouth for a bus terminal and try to park a Number 39 in it. *[To mates]* That is if they haven't already mistaken her for the back end of the bus!

'LAD' 4:   What about you, my darlin'? Was your daddy a burglar, eh?

'GIRL' 3:   What d'you mean?

'LAD' 4:   Well, he must have stolen the stars from the sky to put them in your eyes!

'GIRL' 3:   [Giggles] Well, I don't know about that... bet you say that to all the girls!

'GIRL' 2:   [Butts in] And has anyone ever told you that your eyes are dark pools...

'LAD 4':   [Smirking] Yeah?

'GIRL' 2:   Yeah, pools of puke! [Links arms with 'Girl' 3 and pulls her away]

'LAD' 5:   Nice try. Now watch a master at work. [Saunters over to 'Girl' 4] Hey baby, don't I recognize you? You're a model aren't you?

'GIRL' 4:   [Looks pleased] Oooh no, you must be mistaken, not me. [Giggles] But I'd like to be.

'LAD' 5:   I never mistake a beautiful girl. Oh, but wait, who is your friend? [Points to 'Girl' 2] My mate over there would like to get to know her.

'Lad' 4 shakes head vigorously. 'Lad' 5 addresses 'Girl' 2

                 You see that lad over there, love, well, his tongue's on fire and he needs a cool kiss of life. Can you help him out darlin'?

'GIRL' 2:   You tell your mate I'll give him a kiss anytime he likes. A Glasgow kiss that is! And if he's on fire, I'll take pity... and chuck a bucket of water over him. That should cool him down a bit, eh?

'LAD' 5:   Oof. You are one tough cookie, but as for my little peaches and cream here – [To 'Girl' 4] Shall I see you later then sweetheart? [Pats her bottom]

'GIRL' 4: Ooh, you are cheeky! I'll be looking out for you!

'LAD' 5: *[Goes back to 'lads', makes gesture of victory]* See? Easy. Hey *[To 'Lad' 6]* Your turn! Haven't seen much action from you yet!

'LAD' 6: *[Struts nonchalantly]* All right then. *[Approaches 'Girl' 1]* Get your coat, love... you've pulled. *[Stands back for effect]*

'GIRL' 1: *[Looks him up and down in silence, he shifts uncomfortably]* I don't think so. *[She turns to her friends, all laugh hysterically]*

'LAD' 6: *[Shrugs]* Your loss.

All freeze as bouncers click fingers

Scene 25

Scenes 25 to 28 are optional and can be used with a pick'n'mix approach.

BOUNCER 1: Next scene, next scene.

BOUNCER 2: These 'girls' are really quite extreme.

Improvised scene. 'Girl' 2, the superior type, and 'Girl' 3, the flirt, approach 'lads' in predatory manner and chat them up. Some of the 'lads' are rather nervous.

Scene 26

Bouncers click fingers.

BOUNCER 1: Next, a slick and greasy type.

BOUNCER 2: Specialist in tacky tripe.

BOUNCER 1: This reptile thinks

BOUNCER 2: he's quite a catch,

BOUNCER 1: if only he could

BOUNCER 2: strike

BOUNCER 1: love's match!

LOUNGE LIZARD: *[Girl dressed in shiny suit, with greased-back hair steps forward. Approaches three 'girls']* Ladies, ladies, ladies! Might I not compliment the cut of your clothes, your quintessential curves, your...

'GIRL' 1: *[Interrupts]* Oh, you are sooo smooth...

'GIRL' 2: As an oil slick.

LOUNGE LIZARD: Ladies, please. Calm yourselves. I just came over to offer any assistance in the warming-up department. My hands have been on specialist training courses. My tongue has been entered for the triple jump and my hips, well, my hips are the basis of Greenwich Mean Time. They keep the rhythm and rhyme. *[He bumps and grinds]*

'GIRL' 3: Oh, slimeee!

ALL: Yeuchhhh!

LOUNGE LIZARD: I can see I am causing quite a stir. I seem to have this effect on young chicklings. When I get them on the dance floor, our bodies collide like heavy goods vehicles. We are talking passion pile-up, babies.

'GIRL' 1:   Send for an ambulance!

'GIRL' 2:   This guy needs to be coned off!

'GIRL' 3:   I've got a bad case of the runs!

They all run away

LOUNGE LIZARD: Ladies, overwhelmed by my presence. Sometimes my radiance blinds them. It is so difficult, wearing the weight of my wonderfulness... *[Exits]*

Scene 27

Bouncers click fingers.

BOUNCER 1: But what about the lads,

BOUNCER 2: when they have to use

BOUNCER 1: the rather unsavoury

BOUNCER 2: gentlemen's loos?

Improvised scene. 'Lads' go to loos. Choreographed action of surreptitious comparison, lack of eye contact, forced conversation and ribald comments about the 'girls'.

Scene 28

Bouncers click fingers.

BOUNCER 1: Now, here's a lad, learning a few licks,

BOUNCER 2: about to train for the tongue

BOUNCER 1: oh-lympics!

BOUNCER 2: He's reached that moment, mustn't miss

BOUNCER 1: great success with his very first kiss!

'Lad' and 'girl' in mime, reach imminent kiss moment. 'Lad' is about to nervously kiss 'girl', when he is tapped on shoulder by Trainer in tracksuit and trainers who jogs on spot as he talks, moving energetically

TRAINER: This is the moment you have been waiting for. But are you *really* ready? Really, fully prepared?

'LAD': What?

TRAINER: This is a field for experts. Have you done your training? Have you undergone tongue analysis?

'LAD': You what?

TRAINER: *[Demonstrates]* Just remember, hips and lips, hips and lips.

'Lad' gives it a go, swiveling hips round. 'Girl' stands to side waiting, bored

TRAINER: First warm up.

'LAD': Yeah. I'm ready.

TRAINER: Pout to the snout. Pucker those lips. *[Puts finger in*

lips like child and goes 'wibble, wibble, wibble'. 'Lad'
copies him] Good. Excellent. Love your lips. Nurture
them. They are the sultans of smooch! Tongue out!

'LAD':   Ahhhhh!

TRAINER: Clockwise!

'Lad' moves tongue round
          Anticlockwise!

'Lad' does same
          Now, be daring, improvise. Yeah! Get down that
          gullet! Explore those recesses. Tunnel down those
          tonsils! Furnurgle with those fillings.

'LAD':   [*Really goes for it with the tongue mime then stops,*
          exhausted] I don't think I can do it coach. [*Sticks*
          tongue out again and stares, cross-eyed at it. Mumbles] I
          think I just sprained my tongue...

TRAINER: Stinking thinking! Hold your nerve. [*Cups 'lad' under*
          chin with one hand and mimes poking tongue back in
          with pointed finger. 'Lad's' mouth remains open] Just
          remember, bad breath equals kiss of death. [*Fishes out*
          breath freshener. Mimes using it on 'lad' then pushes up
          chin to close 'lad's' mouth]

'LAD':   All right then. I'm all set. I am *in* the game and
          ready to osculate! [*Turns, confident]*

However 'girl' has got bored and is now miming kissing another
'lad'. First 'lad' walks off, dejected. Bouncers click fingers

BOUNCER 1: Rejection!

BOUNCER 2: Ah, it's such a shame,

BOUNCER 1: but that's enough of our little game.

BOUNCER 2: With a click, our hammy sham

BOUNCER 1: turns ham and cheese

BOUNCER 2: To cheese and ham.

Bouncers click fingers three times and boys and girls resume own genders, swapping back clothes and accessories. They shake themselves, obviously feeling odd and rub necks and shoulders as though waking up befuddled. It is as though they are climbing back into their own bodies

BOUNCER 1: Revels ended, mischief done. We've had our fill of

BOUNCER 2: gratuitous fun.

BOUNCER 1: And after these morsels of

BOUNCER 2: distraction, it's time to catch the finale:

BOTH: *[As film directors]* action!

Scene 29

Scott and Jim are talking as they approach Suzy.

SCOTT: Right, so you know what to do. Got the patter all worked out. I'm your best mate and I'll be right behind you. *[Aside]* Laughing my head off! Let him ruin his chances, then Stell and I can pick up where we left off and poor old Jim can leave us to it. Mean? Me? I prefer to think of it as protecting my best interests.

JIM: *[Breathing like an athlete]* OK, it's now or never. Warp factor five. Full speed ahead! *[Approaches Suzy who is standing at edge of stage with her back to him and the name on the hat clearly visible]* Um, are you busy right now?

SUZY: *[Turns, smiles]* Not at all. I was just waiting to see if anyone could make this birthday one to remember.

JIM: Oh, good. Well, I'll do my best to... oblige... Um, this is dedicated to you. *[Falls on knees. Begins nervously but steadily gains confidence]*
'Come live with me, and be my love,

As he speaks, all characters on stage go silent. With a couple of giggles from girls, they turn and stare. Stella enters and moves near to Scott.

And we shall all the pleasures prove.

That hills and valleys, dales and fields
And all the craggy mountain yields.
And I will make thee beds of roses *[Pulls out a rose and offers it to her]*
With a thousand fragrant posies...
A belt of straw and ivy buds
With coral clasps and amber studs.'

SCOTT: *[Standing with arms crossed, looking smug]* Studs? Yes! Now this *is* poetry.

Rest of assembled cast are enthralled however

ALL: *[Shout]* Shut yer gob Scott!

JIM: 'And if these pleasures may thee move,
Come live with me and be my love.'

SUZY: *[Entranced]* Am I to understand that you're asking me out?

Jim nods

At last! Come here you. *[She helps him up and pulls him into an embrace]*

Everyone erupts in cheers and clapping. Stella watches, disgusted

SCOTT: Blast him! Why's she getting off with Jim?

Scott and Stella both do puking motions. As Stella tips forward, her hat is clearly visible. She meets Scott's eyes from under her hat. They approach each other

SCOTT: You don't approve?

STELLA: Hand me a sick bag.

SCOTT: You surprise me.

STELLA: What they're doing surprises me.

SCOTT: But I thought you weren't like that.

STELLA: Not like THAT, thank you very much.

SCOTT: You're not so woozy after all, are you Suzy!

STELLA: Excuse me? How could you mistake *me* for her?

SCOTT: But then... *[Thinking]* That means you are over there right now, wrapped round Jim AND talking to me! Blimey, Stell. I'm confused.

STELLA: Scott, I don't mind a lad who's stupid, but you are taking a whole shipment of biscuits and delivering them to planet Dim. I wouldn't kiss Jim if his tongue were kebabed in a bap! Anyway, why are we wasting time talking about him? Forget those two, I've got my eyes on a much tastier take-away. *[She grabs Scott in a tango sweep and her hat is swept off in the confusion]*

SCOTT: OK! Let's go super stellar

STELLA: Let's play hot scotch!

They embrace

JIM: *[To Suzy. Leads her forwards]* Stella, you're so warm and... different under that cold shell.

SUZY: *[Takes off hat. Throws it away]* Well, if the hat fits, wear it.

JIM: *[Looks closely]* You're not... *[Realises she's Suzy]*

SUZY: Woozy? No, I'm not, that's Stella's nickname for me. The name is Suzy. Glad to meet you properly, at last. *[She offers hand]*

JIM: Glad to... *[Smiles]* meet you too!

They hold hands

Scene 30

Bouncers step forward. Throughout epilogue, the couples referred to move forwards to mime the action described. Music for the last dance plays. Rest of cast pair up and dance slowly in the background.

BOUNCER 1: Ah! And so that wraps

BOUNCER 2: the vital pairing, with hats and ribbons bold and

BOUNCER 1: daring.

BOUNCER 2: This evening's tangy dollop of laughter

BOUNCER 1: has left our couples

BOUNCER 2: ... ever after.

BOUNCER 1: We left out

BOUNCER 2: 'happy'

BOUNCER 1: for who can see,

BOUNCER 2: beyond this changeling evening spree?

BOUNCER 1: Stella and Scott, both think they're hot.

BOUNCER 2: But are cold inside, and rather snide.

BOUNCER 1: Suzy and Jim, not just a whim,

BOUNCER 2: they deserve a chance,

BOTH: let them have the last dance!

BOUNCER 1: Get-away girl

Girl from scenes 4, 11 and 19 dances by herself, cradling an empty glass

         and sad, sad boy.

Kenneth dances energetically and badly, bopping between couples

BOUNCER 2: Poor loser Kenneth, so very annoy-

BOUNCER 1: ing.

BOUNCER 2: Such a pity he couldn't open his ears

BOUNCER 1: when she tried to pour out her blackout fears.

BOUNCER 2: As for the lads who reckon they're hard?

BOUNCER 1: They hold all the attraction

BOUNCER 2: of rancid old lard.

BOUNCER 1: *[Optional lines referring to Lounge Lizard. Can be cut if not performing scene 26]* But Lounge Lizard there, found a peg for his mac.

BOUNCER 2: She's a tall, skinny beanpole who can't answer back.

BOUNCER 1: She won't run away when he kisses her hand.

BOUNCER 2: The perfect, quiet girlfriend: a hat and coat stand!

Lounge Lizard dances with a coat stand and tips it gently towards him to kiss one of the protruding coat hooks as though it is a hand

BOUNCER 1: Another night of

BOUNCER 2: hopes

BOUNCER 1: and dreams.

BOUNCER 2: Of captivating plots

BOUNCER 1: and schemes

BOUNCER 2: lies dusty, on the emptying floor.

Cast begin leaving the dance floor

BOUNCER 1: But soon they'll all be back for

BOTH: more.

BOUNCER 1: See you tomorrow, next weekend, next week.

BOUNCER 2: For you never quite know when you'll find

BOUNCER 1: what you seek.

BOUNCER 2: Outside it's raining.

BOUNCER 1: In here is warm.

BOUNCER 2: Flirtation's safe refuge that weathers the storm.

BOTH: *[Turn to cast and act as bossy bouncers]* Come on you
           lot: out! Haven't you got homes to go to? Come on.
           Let's be having you. *[To embracing couple]* Spit him
           out love, you don't know where he's been. *[To a
           slumped lad]* Oi, sleepy head, WAKEY, WAKEY.
           Time to go.

*Murmers of farewell, reluctance to leave etc. as cast pick up coats.
Girls' group still have buckets as handbags*

GIRL 1:   But it's pouring outside!

GIRL 2:   My shoes'll be ruined!

GIRL 3:   *[Moves offstage, holding bucket above head]* Eeew, it's
           coming down cats and dogs out here. Hurry UP!

Toy cats and dogs are thrown onto stage

LAD: Woah, see what you mean. But we can keep you
           warm! Come on. Run for it.

GIRL 4:   Let's go.

All exit except bouncers

GIRL 5:   *[Offstage, squeals]* It's BUCKETING down!

Buckets are thrown back onto stage. Bouncers jump then recover their composure. Sounds of laughter, squeals and footsteps fade. Bouncers mime closing doors, turn and stand shoulder to shoulder, facing the audience. They smooth their hair in unison, pick imaginary fluff from jacket sleeves, dust their hands together then fold their arms. Lean towards audience, staring them out

BOUNCER 1: You still here?

Both unfold arms and make identical exit signs with thumbs over shoulders, indicating to them to get out. Fold arms again

BOTH: *[Pointedly]* Good night!

Exit

THE END

Rehearsal and Workshop ideas

Exercises and ways in

The two bouncers perform with synchronised movements for maximum visual impact and to heighten the effect of their lines threading into each other. In pairs, perform a mirroring exercise facing each other, where A leads the movement and B mirrors exactly. Then, change position to stand shoulder to shoulder with an imaginary mirror in between. Practise exact, choreographed movements together.

Buckets feature as a visual running joke. Before reading the text, play the game of 'endless prop' in groups or pairs with buckets. Use the bucket as though it is anything but a bucket. Be as inventive as possible. You may want to incorporate extra uses you devise into the final performance.

There are certain scenes requiring exaggerated performance levels. As a whole group, use the phrase 'I love you' as a script to perform at three different, exaggerated levels: low, medium and high. 'Low' is performed in a very earthy, guttural, deep-voiced, heavy style. 'Medium' is a bland, simple statement, enacted in neutral manner. 'High' is level-ten style exaggeration: as physically and vocally over the top as possible. A leader calls out levels at random. All respond simultaneously, on the spot or moving and delivering the line to each other.

Exaggeration of gender stereotypes is used deliberately to create humour. See stage directions for beginning of scene 9. In pairs, play 'follow my leader', copying and exaggerating each other's walks and mannerisms. Spend time observing each other carefully before copying. Repeat in small groups, with each person exaggerating more than the person in front. Try in larger groups! You should be able to see the increase in exaggeration along the line.

As part of the preparation for the gender-reversal scenes (24-27), play the same 'follow my leader' game, but concentrate on exaggerating stereotypes of how girls and boys walk. See later exercises under character development for extending exaggerated physicalisation of the opposite sex.

Character development

Choose a character from the play. Experiment with becoming that character physically. Without speaking, enact how that character sits, walks, dresses to go out, eats, reads a book or magazine and enters the club.

Try doing these actions first as yourself, then in role, and comment on the differences. Next, work on integrating how your character moves and speaks. In a circle, practise entering and introducing yourself to the group in role. The rest of the group should comment on what messages they pick up about your character from your body language, mannerisms, facial expression, gesture and stance.

When you have practised movements to fully inhabit your chosen character, take it in turns to hot seat each other. In pairs or groups, ask questions that each person must answer in role. Concentrate specifically on how your character communicates using body language and facial expression, as well as words. Observers should comment primarily on what was indicated physically by each character. Look closely at use of hands, position of feet, shoulders and arms in relation to body (open? closed?), angle of head, eye contact and posture.

For the gender swap scenes (24-27), repeat the two previous exercises as your opposite sex. For heightened comic effect, you should aim to recreate and then exaggerate stereotypes and clichés of how males and females move.

Before you attempt to enact the opposite gender, begin by walking around the space as yourself. Notice which muscles you use, where your weight is balanced, how you hold your head and shoulders and how your feet hit the floor. Move on to experimenting with using different body centres to emphasise and lead your walk: how does your walk change if you lead with your forehead, shoulders, chest, hips, ankles or toes? Exaggerate them. Do any of these walking states give you a way into moving as the opposite sex?

Do a whole group improvisation with reversed genders. 'Boys' should try to impress 'girls', who should react appropriately. Dance in role!

Status is important in the roles of the two pairs of characters, Suzy and Stella, and Scott and Jim. Stella and Scott adopt high status and Suzy and Jim have low status.

In pairs, experiment with ways of showing physically who is high and who is low status. Consider in particular use of eye contact, ways of standing and mannerisms.

For Suzy and Stella, devise a set of actions that can be easily repeated. This could be opening a wardrobe door, choosing an item of clothing, discarding it, choosing another, trying it on, posing in front of mirror, choosing an accessory, hearing a phone ring, picking it up or checking a text message. First perform these actions together, concentrating on making similar movements with similar timing. Then, repeat the same actions but work on individual ways of moving that denote character and status. Stella is self-assured. She maintains a detached superiority by moving very precisely. In contrast, Suzy has more nervous mannerisms. Her hands fidget, she's more energetic, and her posture is more closed and defensive.

When performing the text, use some synchronised actions to suggest Stella and Suzy's connection as twins, with the individual characterisations suggesting and highlighting the differences between them. Playing the twins as high and low status indicates to the audience why it is that the sisters can look physically quite similar but be viewed so differently. The performer playing Suzy must then switch physically when she pretends to be Stella in order to make the deception believable to other characters, and also to the audience.

For Scott and Jim, devise and improvise a set of actions based around entering a room, greeting each other and looking in a mirror. As with Stella and Suzy, concentrate on the physical differences in the performance of each action that reveals Scott as the self-assured egomaniac and Jim as the shy, nervous one.

Focus of attention

For the performer playing the girl in scenes 4, 11 and 19, the use of a few carefully chosen objects can be very useful for maintaining a focus for the character's actions while she is revealing something of her inner life.

For the monologues in scenes 11 and 19, in the club, the girl is alone, either seated or standing. Try performing this scene with no props at all.

Then, assemble a few appropriate props and accessories such as handbag plus contents, mobile phone, hair accessory (hair band or clip), necklace, beer mats on a table and an empty glass. Rehearse the scene numerous times, experimenting with what the character is doing while speaking. Is she fiddling with/ripping up beer mats? Removing and replacing a hair accessory? Looking fruitlessly for something in her handbag? Emptying the contents of her handbag onto the table? Fiddling with a necklace? Comment on the difference between performing with and without props.

For scene 4, between Mum and Girl, an ironing board is specified. In pairs, try performing this scene with no props at all (i.e. no ironing board or iron). Repeat with props, (using a table to represent the ironing board and a shoe for the iron if necessary). Discuss the differences between the two presentations of the scene.

Develop the performance of the scene further by using the ironing board as a barrier and obstacle between Mum and Girl that they both move around. For the performer playing Mum, what dimensions/inferences does her use of the iron bring to the scene?

Improvisation

The role of Kenneth is a demanding one in terms of pace, timing of line delivery, his attempts at interaction with others and his manic physical performance. Read through scene 17. Without the text, improvise the gist of this scene, concentrating on his mannerisms, gestures and facial animation, and the reactions of groups and individuals to him.

Scene 15 is based on an improvisation exercise where a short scene is replayed in different ways. In pairs or groups, improvise a short scene where someone is trying to do something that ends in failure. Go through it several times so it can be repeated using exactly the same words and movements. Then:

    1. Perform it as looped dialogue (repeat over and over)

2. Perform it as though a video fast-forward button has been pressed
3. Perform in slow motion
4. Perform the fantasy version where it ends differently
5. Perform it backwards
6. Perform it in different styles e.g. football commentary, melodrama, science fiction.

Scene 25 is an optional scene with limited directions. Improvise this scene after initial gender swap exercises.

TWISTED

Gretel is a fairly average teen: she falls out with her dad and has issues with her boyfriend. But in one way Gretel is different – she is in a coma. How did she get there? In this tale full of twists and turns there is more than one suspect...

KICK OFF

Enter the football-crazy world of Diddlebury Heights: a hypochondriac coach, a pompous headmaster, rapping cheerleaders, a stolen trophy and commentators with puns more disgraceful than the team's pitiful performance. Will the school be saved from the evil developer who has her eye on the very land it is built on?

PLAYS WITH ATTITUDE

FLIPSIDE

Flipside brings a contemporary twist to a trio of folk tales. Meet a host of feisty characters, from an eastern-European Cinderella to Nasrudin, a middle-Eastern fool, as they show us the dangers of judging by appearance alone and the importance of speaking the truth and acting with integrity.